Moon Madness

by
Tim Wall

Watermill Press

Printed in the United States of America

Illustrations by Jim Odbert

ISBN 0-89375-792-6

CONTENTS

MOONQUAKE

Natalie Harrison removed the cake from her oven and took it into the living room.

"Look what's happened," she said to her husband. "My cake fell."

Jay Harrison looked up from the

evening news. His wife was right. The cake had caved in. Large cracks ran across the top of it.

"What am I going to do?" Natalie moaned. "The Riveras will be here in an hour. For weeks, I've been boasting to Jane Rivera about my lemon cake. Now look at it."

Jay Harrison was used to people bringing him problems to solve. He was the chief engineer of Luna City, and he was in charge of the machines that kept the city of twenty thousand people alive.

Luna City was built beneath the surface of the moon. There were machines that made air to breathe. There were machines that sent out heat and light, and there were machines that grew food. All the machines were under the direction of Jay Harrison.

"Put some frosting on the cake," he said to his wife. "No one will be able to tell that it caved in."

"Do you think that would do it?" his wife asked. Before Harrison could answer, he and his wife were knocked to the floor. The lights in the apartment went out.

A moment later, the lights came back on, but they were only half as bright as before. In the dim light, the Harrisons saw that all the furniture in the room had been turned over.

Harrison jumped to his feet. "Are you all right?" he asked his wife. He reached for her arm and helped her up.

"I'm fine," she said, brushing a lock of hair away from her face. "But now look at my cake. It's destroyed."

The cake was now only a pile of crumbs, but Harrison didn't bother to look at it. He was already at the telephone, dialing the city's control center.

"This is Harrison," he said. "What's the report?"

"This is Bogdanov," the voice answered. "We've been hit with a moonquake, sir — a big one. We're on emergency power right now."

Harrison swore under his breath. The moon, like Earth, was sometimes ripped apart by powerful earthquakes. On the moon, though, they were called "moonquakes." And they were even more dangerous than earthquakes. If a quake were to rip open the sealed tunnels of Luna City, the people inside would be helpless.

"This is Harrison," he said. "What's the report?"

"What's happened to the main engines?" Harrison asked.

"The computer shows that the main parts are still in order. I've sent a team out to make repairs. My guess is that they'll need about six hours."

"Good work," Harrison said. "Are there any leaks showing?" He crossed his fingers.

"None so far...hold it. I'm getting a flashing light from Air Lock 6. The seals must be starting to go, although they haven't cracked yet."

"Round up a crew and get them up to Number 6 on the run," Harrison said. "I'm on my way right now."

Harrison kissed his wife and slipped out the door of their apartment. The lights in the tunnel street were dim. People were spilling into the street from their apartments. They milled around in small groups. A buzz of alarmed questions filled the air.

Harrison pushed his way through the crowds. He raced to the corner building where a plain red door faced the street. The sign above the door said "Emergency Only." Harrison took an identification card from his pocket and placed it in the lock. The door opened. He stepped in and punched the button marked "Level 1."

Harrison's legs buckled as the elevator rose at high speed. Before he could stand up straight, the door slid open.

The engineer at Lock 6 looked worried.

"Good evening, Svenson," Harrison said. "What's going on here?"

"Let's go up to the top," the engineer

said. "I'll show you."

The two men stepped into a tall, round tower. A ladder leaned against the wall of the tower. The men climbed upward, arm over arm.

When they reached the top, they were inside one of the bubble windows that looked out over the surface of the moon. Gray, rocky plains stretched all around them. The mountains were far away. The few buildings that stood on the surface of the moon were close by. The air locks were nearby, too. The heavy steel doors of the air locks allowed people to enter and leave Luna City. The city's air, however, was kept sealed in.

"You can see the path of the quake from here," Svenson said, pointing. Harrison saw a huge crack that snaked across the plains. It reached all the way

*Harrison saw a huge crack that snaked
across the plains.*

to Air Lock 6.

"The air locks are very strong," Svenson said. "But this is a direct hit. There are hundreds of tons of rock pressing against that lock. It won't be long before it snaps open. I hate to think what will happen if it does."

In his mind, Harrison could see what would happen. The air in Luna City would rush out like air from a balloon. Then the tunnels would cave in. Luna City would look like the cake his wife had baked.

By the time Harrison and Svenson had climbed back down the ladder, the work team had arrived. Harrison's face showed no sign of worry. If the others saw that he was afraid, the fear would spread. But Harrison was starting to lose hope. He thought again of the cake his wife had made. *Just put some frosting on it*, he had told her. If only this problem could be solved in the same way.

Harrison snapped his fingers. Maybe it could. He called to the captain of the work team.

"I want you to send half your people down to Level 16," he told him. "They'll find tanks of that new chemical we have developed—the one that comes out like rubber. Have them put hoses onto the tanks. Get the other half of your people into suits. I want them ready to go out to the surface. Both groups will meet at Air Lock 5."

Harrison gave further directions. Then the two groups split up. Harrison climbed back to the bubble window with Svenson.

In a little while, workers in silver space suits walked out of Air Lock 5. They carried the large tanks with the hoses. They moved to where the crack in the moon met Air Lock 6.

Following Harrison's orders, the workers slipped the hoses into the cracks outside the air lock. Then the chemical from inside the tanks came pouring out.

After the chemical left the tank, it became a dark, shiny film. Soon the end of the crack nearest Lock 6 was filled. Then the film covered the surrounding ground in a wide circle.

"That puts the frosting on the cake," Harrison said.

"What did you say, sir?" Svenson asked.

"I'm sorry. I'm just talking to myself,"

Harrison said. He picked up the phone in the bubble room and asked for Bogdanov.

"The lights for Lock 6 have stopped flashing," Bogdanov said. "The air lock is safe again."

Harrison turned to Svenson. "Even if the lock cracks, the air will stay in," he said. "We won't be able to use Lock 6 again. But that's a small price to pay for staying alive."

Harrison picked up the phone again. This time, he punched out the number for his own apartment.

"I'm sorry I had to leave in such a hurry," he said to his wife. "There was a problem I had to take care of."

"You're still not too late for dinner," Natalie Harrison said. "The Riveras just called. They'll be over in ten minutes.

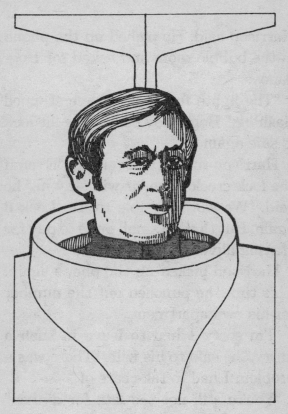

*"Even if the lock cracks, the air will stay in,"
Harrison said.*

I've cleaned up the apartment, and the pot roast is done. But there won't be anything for dessert."

"That's fine with me," Harrison said. "I don't think I could face a lemon cake right now anyway."

The Thief of Baghdad

"Really, there's no reason to worry," Mr. Murdoch said. He leaned back in his chair and laced his fingers together over his chest. "The Luna City Bank is as safe as any bank you'll find on Earth—maybe safer."

A stranger faced Mr. Murdoch across

a wide desk. He had tan skin and a straight, sharp nose like the beak of a hawk. Black eyebrows arched across his forehead. Murdoch admired the well-tailored suit the stranger wore.

"I suppose you're right," the stranger said. "But I feel I must be careful. I'm used to doing business in places like New York and Tokyo and London. These settlements on the moon seem so wild and new. I have to be sure my family's money will be safe."

"Of course, Mr. Cane. But I'm sure you'll find Luna City a wonderful place to do business." Then Murdoch gave a sly smile. "For a man like you, young and full of ideas, there's a lot of money to be made."

"That's what I hope for," Mr. Cane said. "Still, I hear a lot of talk back on

"*I have to be sure my family's money is safe,*"
the stranger said.

Earth. What about this man they call 'The Thief of Baghdad'?"

Murdoch sat forward and waved a hand in the air. "He's a smalltime crook — the sort that picks the pockets of visitors at the Hotel Copernicus. I'm afraid that newspapers have given him more glory than he deserves. Surely you don't believe everything you read in the papers?"

"No, of course not," Cane replied. "But they say he's very smart. Why has he never been caught?"

"It's only because of the part of the city he comes from, Mr. Cane. As you know, Luna City is a web of streets and tunnels built below the ground. One part of the city is known as 'Baghdad.'

"People of all nationalities live in Baghdad. It's very crowded — a maze of

23

shops, tunnels, and small apartments. It's really quite interesting. You'll have to visit it yourself...in the company of a friend, of course."

Murdoch smiled. Then he continued, "This man, who has come to be known as 'The Thief of Baghdad,' is somehow always able to make his escape into this maze."

"Well, I'm not sure," said Mr. Cane. "I have a lot of valuables to deposit. I just don't know if Luna City is safe enough."

"Mr. Cane, would you allow me a few minutes of your time? I think I can ease some of your worries."

Murdoch pressed a button at the side of his desk. "Ms. Juarez, I'll be out of my office for a moment. Please hold my calls." He pressed another button. Part of the wall behind him slid open. The

*Murdoch pressed a button at the side
of his desk.*

banker motioned to Cane. "Please, fol-
low me."

They walked down a smooth, white
hall. Murdoch tapped at a spot that
seemed as smooth as any other. Again,
part of the wall slid away without a
sound.

"We have a special safe built to hold
valuables such as yours," Murdoch said
as they walked down another hall.

"Bars made of gold mined from the
asteroid belt are kept here as well as
jewels that were discovered on Mars.
And of course, we have several of the
'Moon Diamonds' that were found just
outside Luna City."

They came to a heavy steel door set
into one wall. Shoulder-high to Murdoch
was a black circle. He placed his hand
against it.

"Notice how this door works," Murdoch said. "It will open only when it senses the prints of all five of my fingers. As a matter of fact, I'm one of the only people who can open this door." The door swung open and the two men stepped into darkness. Then Murdoch flicked on a light switch.

Gold, silver, and bright white diamonds gleamed from inside glass trays. The trays covered all four walls of the room. Murdoch looked proud. "Now don't you feel better, Mr. Cane?"

"I certainly do." With a quick step, Cane was in front of a stack of trays. In an instant, he scooped up a handful of diamonds. Then he shoved them into the pocket of his suit.

"Just what do you think —?" Murdoch started to say. But before he could

"Notice how this door works," Murdoch said.

finish, Cane had pushed him away from the door.

"I'm afraid I'll have to lock you in your safe," Cane said. "But you won't have to stay for long. As soon as I've escaped, I'll let Ms. Juarez know where she can find you."

"You won't get far," Murdoch said. "I warn you, Cane. The hotels will be searched. The ships leaving Luna City will be watched."

"My name's not Cane," the man said. "And I don't have far to go—just back to my friends in Baghdad."

SPACE PROSPECTOR

"I'm telling you, Luke. These claim jumpers aren't fooling around. They'll kill if they have to," Sam said with concern. "A man your age shouldn't be out working by himself."

Luke Sebastian shook his head. He had a wrinkled face, white hair, and a short white beard. But his dark eyes were clear and sharp. "I've been prospecting the asteroid belt for thirty-five years on my own," he said proudly. "I'm not going to change my ways now, and I'm surely not going to stop."

Between the paths of Jupiter and Mars lay the asteroid belt. These pieces of rock were said to be what was left of a world that exploded millions of years ago. Most of the asteroids were huge, worthless rocks. But some held deposits of gold and silver. Others were made up of the very light metals used to build spaceships.

Luke worked like other prospectors in the asteroid belt. He traveled in a small spaceship, testing each asteroid he came across for traces of gold, silver, and other valuable metals. The ones

*"I'm not going to change my ways now,"
Luke Sebastian said.*

with deposits were marked with radio guides. Later, the deposits would be sold to a mining company.

"How do these claim jumpers work?" Luke asked his friend.

"Well, it seems they can track down the asteroids that have radio guides. An advance team destroys the guide. Then the main ship moves in. They hook the asteroid and tow it to a new place. There's no way the prospector can prove his claim."

"Can't the Guard ships do anything?" Luke wondered.

"It seems not," Sam explained. "These claim jumpers move fast. The nearest Guard ship could be millions of miles away. By the time you call one in, the claim jumpers are long gone."

"Sounds like a smart crew," said Luke.

33

"Smart — and nasty. I wish you'd change your mind, Luke. You're not as young as you used to be. You should get out of the business before you get hurt."

Luke sighed. "Sam, my great-grandfather was a prospector back on Earth, in the Rocky Mountains. He fought off wild animals, the cold, and outlaws. And he worked until he was ninety years old. Why should I quit? I'm in the prime of my life."

Luke thanked Sam for the visit. Then Sam returned to his own ship. He was a prospector, too.

Luke's work went on the same as always — until he made a return visit to asteroid K-1525.

The asteroid looked like a mountain of rock floating in cold black space. Earlier, Luke had found large metal deposits on K-1525 and had left a radio guide to mark it. Now the radio signals were dead. And Luke was investigating.

Luke set his ship on a flat part of the asteroid. He got into his space suit and left the ship to search the surface. Then he found the radio guide. It had been crushed into a pile of metal and loose wires. Claim jumpers had hit K-1525.

Luke was angry as he climbed back into his ship. He pulled a dozen blasting charges from his tool box. From under the seat by the steering board, he took the burst gun he kept hidden there. Luke held it to the light and checked its parts.

The claim jumpers, he knew, would move in from the side of K-1525 that faced the sun. It was simpler to see the asteroid that way. So, with the ship's power drive in low, Luke jockeyed until the asteroid was between him and the sun. If he parked in the shadow of the rock, they wouldn't see him and he wouldn't show up on their screens.

Luke zipped up his suit securely and strapped the burst gun and blasting charges to his waist. Then he slipped out the air lock and into space. Only a snaking cord held him to the ship.

Luke looked around at the stars. They were sharp points of light that never twinkled. Then he saw the ship—the claim jumpers. It drifted forward like a shadow. Then it stopped, hanging without motion and without sound. Looking at it over the rim of K-1525, Luke could see every mark on its surface.

Three white-suited figures popped out through the ship's air lock. Using jet

Only a snaking cord held Luke to the ship.

packs, they sped toward the asteroid. They pulled a thick tow line with them.

Now it was time for Luke to make his move. He switched on the radio inside his suit.

"This is Guard ship *Sting Ray*," Luke announced over the radio. "We are checking unknown vessels. Please give your call number. Repeat...please radio your number."

Luke knew they wouldn't answer. Such a ship wouldn't be in the records. But he'd have to give them a scare before they noticed that no Guard ship showed on their screen.

He set one of the charges and tossed it toward the claim jumpers' ship. Moments later, the charge went off in a blinding shower of red and orange. It was so close to the ship that it would

*Luke watched the figures in space suits hurry
back to their ship.*

show up on the ship's screen as one of the Guard's homing rockets. Luke sent off the remaining charges. In a few seconds, the sky was filled with light.

Luke watched the figures in space suits hurry back to their ship. Its power drive glowed, then it was gone.

Luke switched his radio off and laughed as he planted a new radio guide on K-1525. Then he pulled himself back to the air lock and into his ship.

It's about time I get some sleep, Luke thought at last. Settling back in a chair, he laughed again. "I haven't had this much fun since my last trip to Luna City," he said out loud.

LUNA CITY BLUES

I jumped ship as soon as we docked at Luna City. The chief engineer and I just hadn't hit it off. That can get to you in the close quarters of a long space trip.

The papers I had signed said I still

had a lot of time to work off on the spaceship. That meant they could call the Guard and have me dragged back. With this in mind, I headed from the port to the main part of the city. I had one destination—anywhere I could make a quick dollar.

I decided that the best thing to do would be to check out the Hotel Copernicus. It's the only hotel in Luna City. Most of the people that have just arrived stay at the Copernicus. Usually, they don't know how to handle the low weight we have on the moon—for themselves or their bags. And they don't know how to work the elevators.

I figured I could make some change by carrying bags. The first guest that came by was a young lady. She said she had come to take a job as a computer

*I had one destination—anywhere
I could make a quick dollar.*

clerk. She had dark hair and a pretty smile.

This was her first trip away from Earth, she said. She seemed excited and scared and shocked all at once.

On the way up in the elevator, I told her a little about my life in space — about being a freight hand and about a few of my adventures. Some of what I said was even true. She seemed to think it was all strange and wonderful.

She said her name was Astrid. I told her mine was Ulysses S. Jones. At one point, not being used to the low gravity, she almost fell over. I caught her. She looked at me with wide eyes as I held her. Then she blushed and thanked me and went into her room.

Later on in the hotel lobby, one of the real bellboys cornered me. He wasn't too happy about me taking his business. When he started to move in on me, I decided to move on.

I followed the tubes until I came to a game hall. It had computer games, three–D booths, and plenty of players. I walked to the back of the hall, where the pool tables were.

Pool was invented back on Earth. But the game had changed a bit when it came to the moon. Now, there were more sides to the table, more balls, and more pockets. In the low weight, you could make a pool stick do things that Minnesota Fats never dreamed of doing.

There were two rough-looking guys at one of the back tables. They asked if I cared for a friendly game. I said I would but first they should explain to me which end of the stick you push the ball

There were two rough-looking guys at one of the back tables.

with. They promised to show me. Then they asked if I wanted to make the game more interesting. They said we could play Three Man. We'd each put some money in. They would even match me two to one. So I laid out the money I had made at the hotel.

I let them each sink a few balls. I'm not the kind of guy who hogs all the fun. Then I ran eight in a row. I finished with an around-the-corner, triple breakaway, grand slam drop-in. It's a nice shot. It ends with seven balls falling into seven pockets at the same time.

I thanked them for the game. As they had promised, I said, it had been both friendly and interesting. I cleared the money off the edge of the table and started to walk away — all in little more than a second.

47

The two guys looked at each other. Their faces turned angry. I was afraid they might be bad sports, so I quickly footed it to the tube outside the game hall.

The two men followed. They were getting angrier by the second. I tried to walk fast, but I didn't want to run. I didn't want to draw attention. Someone might call for the Guard. And that was the last thing I wanted. On the other hand, I couldn't just stand around and let those two guys catch up with me. They were looking like worse sports all the time.

I turned the corner and headed into the crowd. Then I saw Astrid walking right toward me. She was looking up and down and around, taking in the sights.

I caught her arm and pulled her to the side of the tube. Then I tilted her chin up and kissed her. I held it like that until I heard pounding footsteps go by, plus a few seconds more just to be sure. Then I let go.

For a moment, Astrid had that same wide-eyed look she had when I held her in the hotel. Then she pulled herself together. "I suppose you do this with all the girls you meet," she said.

"I don't know what came over me," I said. I felt in my pocket. The money was still there. "But since it's dinner time, we may as well get something to eat. I know a little place that's pretty good. They have dancing. Dancing on the moon is quite an experience."

Astrid seemed to like the idea in spite of herself. "I don't know what to say,"

"I suppose you do this with all the girls you meet," Astrid said.

she said.

"You don't have to say anything." I put my arm through hers. "Just tell me what you like on the menu. I'll take care of the rest."

A Sense of Danger

There was no chance for Steven McNeil to see the men who attacked him. He had just walked out the door of the Hotel Copernicus, where he had checked in that morning. The street was full of Saturday afternoon crowds. Someone had bumped into McNeil, pushing him into an alley that ran behind the Hotel. Then someone else stepped behind him and knocked him to the ground.

As McNeil fell, he dropped the small leather case he had been carrying. A hand reached out and took the case from the ground in front of him. By the time McNeil picked himself up, the men were gone. So was the case.

McNeil went to the nearest Guard station. He told the officer at the desk what had happened. He also told him why he thought his case had been robbed. The officer said McNeil should speak with Captain Garcia.

Captain Garcia was a short, round man with black hair and a black mustache. He sat behind a desk in a small office. His hands were folded

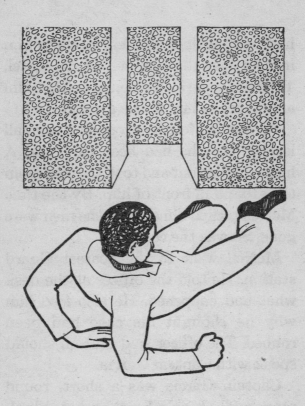

*By the time McNeil picked himself up,
the men were gone.*

across his chest as he leaned back in a chair.

"I'm sure they were trying to steal the papers I had in my case," McNeil told the captain. "Those papers would be worth a lot to anyone who knew where to take them. They describe a new way to separate atomic metals from rock. It took me years of study to discover how it could be done."

Captain Garcia listened to McNeil with his eyes almost closed. For a moment, McNeil thought the man had fallen asleep.

Then the captain opened one eye. "You said these men *tried* to steal your papers?" he asked.

"That's right," McNeil said. "They took my case. But the papers weren't in it. I had left them in my hotel room."

"Who do you think wants these papers?" Garcia asked.

"I don't know," said McNeil. "I thought the Guard was supposed to find out things like that." McNeil was surprised to find his voice becoming sharp. Captain Garcia didn't seem very interested in his problem. McNeil quieted his voice and tried to make himself calm.

"I don't know anyone in Luna City," he said. "I just arrived from Earth last night. I have a meeting with the New World Mining Company on Monday. I'm going to show them my plans—if I still have them. If they want my discovery, they'll pay me a good sum of money for the right to use it."

"Wouldn't some mining company other than New World find your plans

"Who do you think wants these papers?"
Garcia asked.

rather interesting?" Garcia asked.

"Interesting, yes," McNeil said, "—and valuable. There are dozens of mining businesses here on the moon that would like to find a cheaper way to mine atomic metals."

"Are there many people who know about your work?" Garcia asked.

"I've written about my findings for several science reviews," McNeil said. "Just the main ideas, of course. Anyone who was interested could have read about them. As I've said, many businesses would pay a high price for my work."

Garcia nodded. "Any of those things are possible. On the other hand, it's also possible that no one is after your plans, Mr. McNeil. Someone tried to rob you of a traveling case while you were in Luna

City. Such things happen all the time, I'm sorry to say."

"Two or three men wanted to rob me of nothing more than a leather case?" McNeil asked. His voice was rising again. "That doesn't make any sense. I tell you, someone is after my plans."

"I'm afraid there isn't much we can do for you right now," Captain Garcia said. "If you wish to file a report on your stolen case, you should. We'll let you know if it turns up. But we're too busy keeping track of the crimes that have already happened to worry about those that *might*."

McNeil walked out of Garcia's office. *That captain is a fool*, he said to himself. *A major crime is being planned, and the captain will do nothing to stop it.*

McNeil caught one of the tube cars

which carried passengers around Luna City. Slowly, his anger died away, but in its place came fear. It was clear that McNeil would have to take care of himself. He would have to protect his papers from thieves. *But who are the thieves?* McNeil thought. He had no idea. *And how will I protect myself? Those robbers might even try to harm me in order to get my papers.*

He had left the papers in his hotel room. *Someone might be breaking in right now,* he thought. *They might have taken them while I was wasting time with Captain Garcia.*

McNeil got off the tube car when it came to his stop. He hurried up to his room and pulled open a dresser drawer. Then he let out a sigh. The papers were still where he had left them.

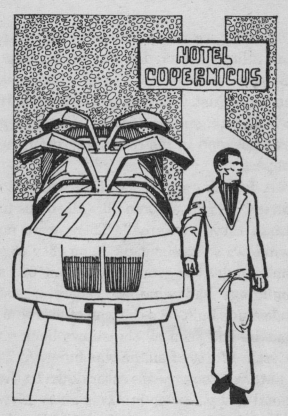

*McNeil got off the tube car when
it came to his stop.*

McNeil stretched out on his bed, feeling a little better. He was on his own. But he would show those robbers he could be just as smart as they were. It would be a simple matter of spending the weekend in his room, guarding the papers.

A few hours later, McNeil wasn't so happy. His hotel room, like all rooms in Luna City, was small. There were no windows to look out of. Luna City was built under the ground, and none of its buildings had windows. There was a television built into the wall of his room, but he had seen all the shows back on Earth. Worst of all, he was hungry.

McNeil took the elevator down to the hotel lobby. *A few minutes away from my room won't matter,* he told himself. He would get something to eat, maybe buy a book to read.

As he crossed the lobby, McNeil noticed a small, sharp-faced man. He was sitting in the lobby, reading a newspaper. But it seemed that the man was also watching McNeil out of the corner of his eye.

McNeil had a hurried meal in the hotel restaurant. As he returned to his room, he saw that the little man was still in the lobby.

The weekend passed slowly. McNeil left his room only to eat. And each time he went out, he saw the man he had noticed on Saturday. But McNeil's papers stayed safe in his room.

McNeil was never so happy to have a weekend go by. He got up on Monday morning, showered, and shaved. All he had to do was get to the New World

Mining Company with his papers. Then he would be safe.

He stopped smiling when he left the hotel. The sharp-faced man was behind him, walking toward McNeil.

A small, electric taxi slid up to the hotel door. McNeil jumped into the cab. He gave the driver the address of New World. As the taxi sped away, McNeil turned around in time to see the little man wave to a black car. It shot into the street behind the cab.

McNeil leaned forward to tell his driver to speed up, but the taxi had already turned down a small side street. From under his jacket, the driver took out a stun pistol.

"Hand me that case, Mr. McNeil," the driver said as he pulled to the curb.

McNeil's heart sank. He had been

"Hand me that case, Mr. McNeil,"
the driver said.

fooled. Just then, the black car following them turned down the same street. There was nothing McNeil could do.

The black car screeched to a stop next to the cab. Two men stepped out of it. One of them was short and round, with a black mustache. He was Captain Garcia.

In two quick steps, Garcia was at the window next to the taxi driver. Garcia also had a stun pistol.

"You can put that gun away," Garcia said in a polite voice. "One of my men will take you downtown."

The driver dropped his stun pistol with a surprised look on his face. McNeil got out of the taxi. His knees felt weak, but he still had his case.

"There's another one," he shouted to Garcia. "Don't let him get away. He's short, with a face like a rat. He's very dangerous."

Captain Garcia laughed. "The man you are talking about," he said, "works for me. He's one of my best officers. I've had him watching you ever since you came to my office."

McNeil's head felt as if it were spinning. This was too much to understand all at once. "You mean you believed what I told you all along?" he asked.

"Yes, I believed what you feared was possible," Garcia said, "enough to put a man on your case. But since we had no idea who the thieves were, it would have been difficult to guard you for the entire weekend. This way, *you* were on your guard. If you had known I had a man watching you, you might have given away that fact to the crooks. I wanted them to make their move while they thought you were on your own."

Garcia's officer was leading the taxi driver away. Garcia shouted some orders to him. Then he turned back to McNeil.

"You have an important meeting to attend," he said. "The New World building is on the way to my office. I'll drop you off at their door, if you like."

McNeil was only five minutes late for his meeting. The New World Mining Company paid him quite well for the rights to his papers.

McNeil returned to Earth the next day. He never went back to Luna City again. But he always remembered his adventure there. And when he told the story to his friends, he never called Garcia a fool.

A Favor
in Return

When I'm in Luna City, I spend most of my time in a game room. I like playing at the pool tables. With a few well-placed bets, I can win a little bit of spending money.

The freight ship I was working on had

landed at Luna City two days before. The ship had gone to Earth, loaded with metal ore, and had returned with its hold full of food. It would be a week before the freight ship took off again.

On the day the Guard came looking for me, I was in a game room shooting pool. An officer entered the room just as I sank two balls in a side pocket.

"I'm looking for Ulysses S. Jones," he said in a loud voice. Someone in the crowd pointed to where I was standing.

I had no idea why the police were looking for me. And I didn't want to stay and find out. So I turned and slipped out the back door of the game room.

The door led to a back alley—where a Guard officer stepped out in front of me. His stun pistol was pointing directly at my chest.

*The freight ship I was working on had landed
at Luna City.*

"You must be Ulysses Jones," he said. He gave me a crooked smile. "Just come along with me."

We joined the other officer in the street. The two of them marched me toward Guard headquarters.

"What's the problem?" I asked the first officer.

"No problem," he said. "The captain just wants to have a talk with you."

"That's very friendly of your captain," I said. "However, I'm a little busy today. Maybe he could invite me over some other time."

"Just keep walking," the officer snarled.

We didn't have anything else to say. At headquarters, one of them led me into Captain Garcia's office. Garcia had a wide face, a clipped black mustache, and was a little thick around the stomach. He was reading a piece of paper as we came in the door.

"You can go now, Magnus," he said. Then he went back to looking at the piece of paper.

"I've just been reading a report on you, Mr. Jones," the captain said. "It seems you've been holding card games in your hotel room. You know that it's against the law to play cards for money in a public building."

"Those card games are just between friends," I said.

"I'm sure they are," Captain Garcia agreed. "Still, you can be locked up for three months because of them. It also says here that you jumped ship six months ago. You broke your signed agreement with the freight company you worked for."

"I can explain that," I said. I didn't like the way our little talk was turning out.

"You can explain it to the judge," Garcia said. "But you're still likely to get thirty days. And then there's the little matter of —"

"You don't have to go on, Captain," I said. I was starting to become angry. "I get the idea. You want to lock me up and throw away the key."

"No, that's not what I want to do." Garcia leaned forward. He stared at me with bright black eyes. "I want to do you a favor. I want to forget about these silly little things. Of course, I expect that you would do me a favor in return."

Alarm bells were going off inside my head. "What kind of a favor?" I asked.

"I want you to help me catch the men

who are bringing these to Luna City." Garcia opened a drawer. He laid two short, deadly-looking pistols on top of his desk. They were made of black shiny metal. The barrel of each gun became wide at the end.

"Those are blast guns," I said.

Garcia nodded. "They send out a force field twenty-five feet wide. Anyone in the path of the field is knocked over. At short distances, the gun can kill. More and more of these blast guns have been turning up in Luna City. My job is to keep them out."

"That's fine," I said. "But I don't understand what all this has to do with me."

"I'm coming to that," Garcia said. "You see, these guns are being shipped to Luna City from Earth. We do not

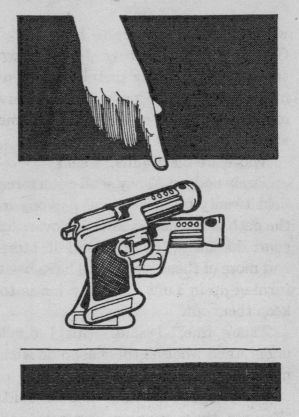

"Those are blast guns," I said.

allow such weapons to be made here on the moon. Someone is secretly running them in by rocket. We even have a pretty good idea of who the gunrunners are. They're connected with a freight line called Two Worlds Shipping. Now, I know that you've worked on many freight ships. You know the docks in Luna City. No one would be surprised to see you working there.

"I want you to get a job loading freight for the company that I'm watching. You're a smart man, Mr. Jones. If you keep your eyes open, you can find out when the guns are being brought in. Then you call me. That's all. Just make sure I'm called before the guns are sent out to be sold on the street."

Now I was starting to worry. Gunrunners are dangerous. "I still don't get it," I said. "You have fifty officers working under you, so you can break in on that freight company any time you want. Why do you need me?"

"I've already tried raids," Garcia said, "but there's always a tip-off ahead of time. The guns are gone before I get there. I believe someone on the Guard is being paid off. I don't know which of my own officers I can trust. Now you see why I need you."

I saw it, but I didn't like it.

"You're trying to make a hero out of me," I said. My voice was bitter.

"Being a hero isn't so bad," Garcia said. "It's better than going to jail."

I wasn't so sure, but I wound up agreeing to take the job. Captain Garcia is a hard man to argue with.

I left Garcia, and caught a tube car to

the port. When I got there, things were as busy as ever. Electric tractors with powerful lift arms moved back and forth. They carried packing crates of all shapes and sizes.

It wasn't hard to get a job with Two Worlds Shipping. I have a friend who works in the port hiring hall. The next day, I was on the job.

I drove one of the tractors with the arm lifts. I worked under a man called Stanley Kosrak. He was big, with thick arms, a wide neck, and a bullet-shaped head. When he shouted orders, he bellowed like an angry bull.

I didn't notice anything important until my fifth day on the job. I was driving a heavy crate into the hall where the freight was stored. The words "Machine Parts" were painted in big, black letters on the side of the crate.

"Take that into the back of the hall," Kosrak shouted to me.

"What for?" I asked. "It's already crowded back there."

"Take it to the back, and don't argue," Kosrak roared. I drove to the back of the hall and finally found a place to leave the crate.

When I was through for the day, I headed for the tube cars. Instead of getting on, though, I circled behind the Two Worlds building. I hid behind a stack of boxes until the guard went past. Then I went in the back door. In a minute, I had climbed to where I had left the crate marked "Machine Parts."

I used my knife to pull two of the boards of the packing crate loose. Inside the crate were racks that held rows and

"Take that into the back of the hall,"
Kosrak shouted.

rows of shiny black pistols. They were the same make as the guns Garcia had in his desk.

I was so busy with the crate that I forgot to pay attention to what was going on around me. Then I heard a voice I knew only too well. It was Kosrak. His words came from behind a nearby pile of sacks.

"We should move the guns out right away," he was saying. "There's a new man working here I don't like. He asks too many questions."

That was enough for me. I raced for the back door and pushed my way out.

For the second time that week, I ran into a Guard officer. It was Magnus, the same officer who had picked me up behind the game room.

"Good thing you came along," I said.

"We've got to call Garcia. The guns have just been shipped in."

Magnus pulled back a big fist and hit me across the face. I slammed into the side of the building, then fell to the ground. Magnus pulled out a gun and moved in on me. He looked at me with that crooked smile.

Then he fell over on his face. Behind him stood Captain Garcia, a stun pistol in his hand. Behind Garcia were three other Guards.

"Aren't you a little early?" I asked him. "I haven't even put a call through yet."

Garcia pulled me to my feet. "I had guessed that Magnus was the one being paid off," he said. "I've been watching him very closely. This afternoon, I noticed he had left his post. The gang most

83

likely called him in to protect them until they had sent out the guns. Then I called your hotel. They said you were late in returning to your room. I decided it was time for me to move in.

"I arrived just in time to see Magnus attack you. I sent one group of my men to the front of the building. I wanted to take care of this one by myself." He poked Magnus, knocked out by the stun pistol, with the toe of his boot. "All in all, everything turned out well."

"I'm glad you think so," I said. "If you ever want me to risk my life again, just let me know."

Garcia smiled in a polite way. "I'm sorry I had to push you around," he said. "I hope you won't hold it against me. When I'm finished here, perhaps you'd care to join me for a game of cards." Garcia winked at me. "Just a little game between friends, you know."

I turned down his offer. Ulysses S. Jones knows enough not to play cards with anyone as smart as Captain Garcia.

SHORT CUT

With Johnny Falcon, you don't know where you're going until you get there. He found me in Luna City, a few weeks after I had jumped a freight ship. I wasn't looking for him. I don't usually go looking for trouble.

"I need another hand for a quick run to Mars," he said. He had found me in the coffee shop of the Hotel Copernicus. The last time I had seen him was in a card game in the part of Luna City called Baghdad.

"No," I said. "Forget it. Remember what happened when I signed with you before? Running out of fuel in the asteroid belt isn't my idea of fun."

"This is different, Ulysses," Johnny said. "I've got big money behind me this time. They're short on machine parts on Mars. If we can get a load to Mars within a certain amount of time, there's a thousand extra in it for both of us."

"What's this 'we' business?" I said.

"Oh, come on. You're not doing anything else right now."

I should have paid for my coffee right

then and left. The trouble was—I didn't have enough to pay for it. We took off from the moon two hours later.

Johnny always seems to look as if he's twenty years old. He wears his hair greased back, and has a boy's good-looking face. His ship was an old Star Stallion XJK. It was small but very fast. Johnny had opened up the back so it could hold freight. Then he had taken the power drive apart and put it back together for more speed. He pampered that ship as if it were his sweetheart.

When we were in free flight, I asked Johnny what our course was.

"Over the sun," he said. That was Johnny's idea of a short cut.

Mars, like Earth, orbits the sun. The easy way to reach Mars would have been to enter its orbit and catch up with

Johnny always seems to look as if he's twenty years old.

it in a wide circle. But Johnny wanted to cut straight across the circle to get to Mars. That would save time. It would also take us right past the sun.

"You're out of your mind," I said. "That's never been done before."

"Unless we take that course, we won't make it to Mars in time to earn the extra thousand."

"An extra thousand," I pointed out, "won't do us much good if we're baked like two potatoes."

"Oh, come on," Johnny said. "That thousand is what you signed up for in the first place."

See what I mean about Johnny Falcon being trouble?

There wasn't much for me to do on a trip like this. I made sure the freight was laid in and safe. After that, I just tinkered around. I looked over the power drive system. I knew something about it from watching engineers on bigger ships. Then I helped Johnny make some calculations for the course we were taking.

It got hot as we neared the sun. First we started sweating. Then it was hard to breath. Finally, Johnny passed out.

Getting hot wasn't the only trouble with being that close to the sun. The sun has a strong pull on anything near to it. In our case, we were very near to it.

By the time Johnny dropped to the floor, I could see the sun through the ship's view port. Soon it was a huge, fiery ball filling up the window. The sun was drawing us in.

Hot and weak, I pulled myself to the steering board. Once, I had watched the

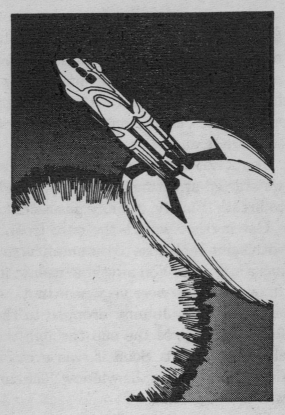

The sun was drawing us in.

captain of a freight ship work the controls. I thought of that now as I tried a few buttons on the board. The sun kept getting bigger. I tried the same buttons again, but in a different order. Then I pulled back on the throttle.

You've got to hand it to Johnny. He kept that power drive in shape. When I pulled the throttle back, I felt a kick. I was pressed back into the seat.

It seemed like days before it was cool enough to breath again. When Johnny came to, we could see Mars in the view port. "We're almost there," I told Johnny, "no thanks to you."

Johnny was his old self in a matter of minutes. "I'll land her," he said. "Then I have another job lined up for us—hauling a special rocket fuel to Station Galileo. The pay is high because there's

"Forget it," Ulysses said.

a small chance it will explode—very small, you understand. It's nothing to worry about."

"Forget it," I said. "After this trip, all I want to do is draw my old-age pay."

Johnny looked hurt. "And all this time I haven't said anything about the three thousand you owe me from that card game."

That's what I mean about Johnny Falcon. You don't know where you're going until you get there.